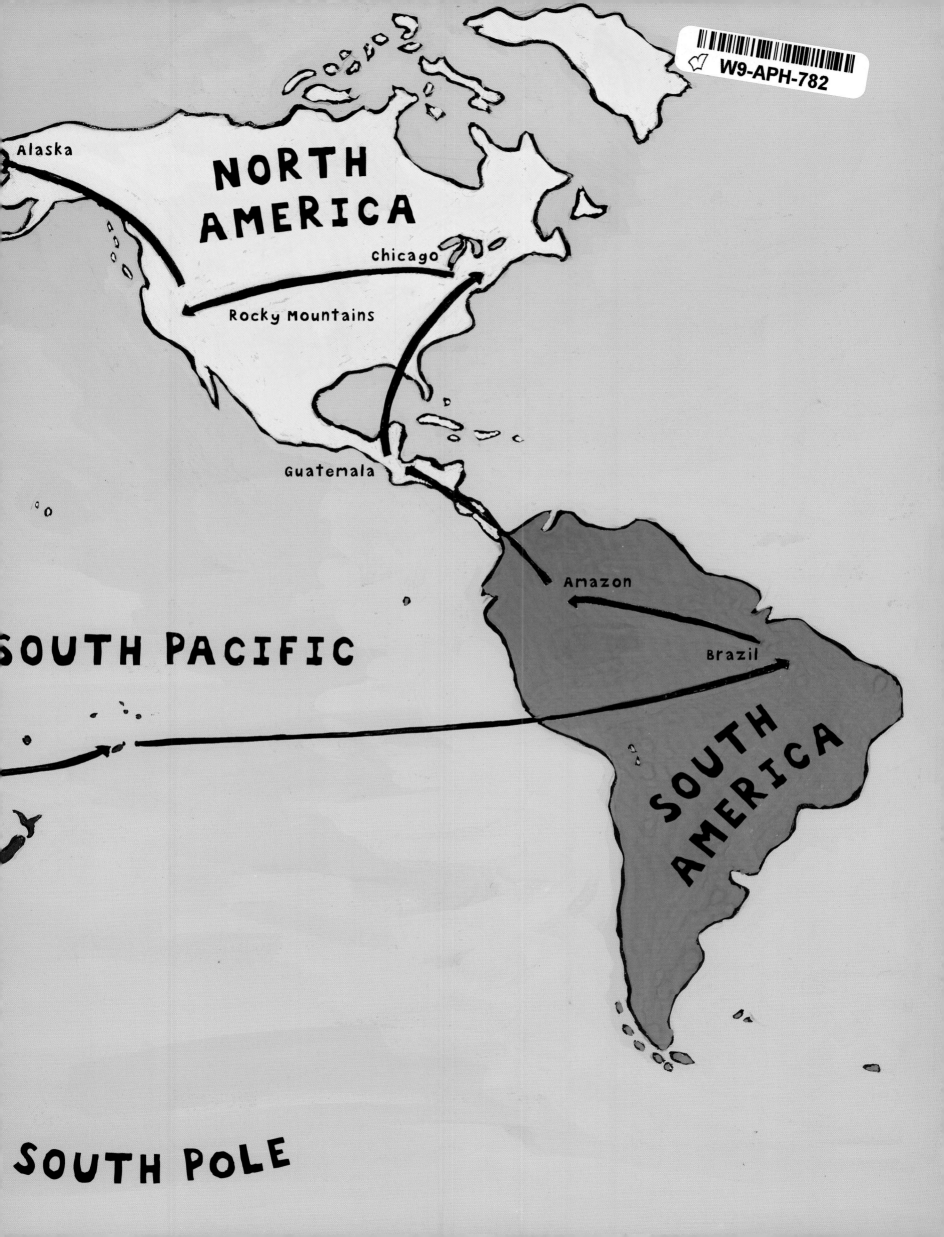

First published in the United States in 2003 by Chronicle Books LLC.

English text design by Jessica Dacher.
Typeset in Bokka, Stone Sans and Meta Plus.
The illustrations in this book were rendered in gouache.
Manufactured in Singapore.

Library of Congress Cataloging-in-Publication Data
Eduar, Gilles.
Gigi and Zachary's around-the-world adventure: a seek-and-find game / Gilles Eduar.
p. cm.
Originally published in France in 2002 by Albin Michel Jeunesse. Summary: On their trip
around the world, Gigi the Giraffe and Zachary the Zebra visit many places and see
many things which the reader is encouraged to seek in the accompanying pictures.
ISBN 0-8118-3909-5
[1. Giraffe—Fiction. 2. Zebras—Fiction. 3. Voyages and travels—Fiction.
4. Picture puzzles. 5. Vocabulary.]
I. Title: Gigi and Zachary's around-the-world adventure. II. Title.
PZ7.E2494 Ar 2003
[E]--dc21
2002007869

Distributed in Canada by Raincoast Books
9050 Shaughnessy Street
Vancouver, British Columbia V6P 6E5

10 9 8 7 6 5 4 3 2 1

Chronicle Books LLC
85 Second Street
San Francisco, California 94105

www.chroniclekids.com

To Sophie, Gérard and all the story-
tellers of la rue Boissonade -G. E.

GIGI AND ZACHARY'S
Around-the-World Adventure

A Seek-and-Find Game

by Gilles Eduar

chronicle books · san francisco

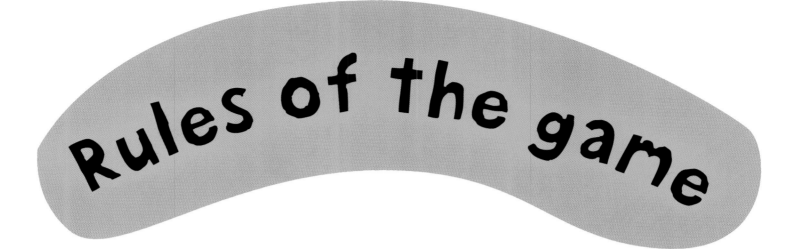

Rules of the game

Gigi the giraffe and Zachary the zebra are taking a trip around the world. At each stop there is a whole universe to explore: beautiful scenery, unusual animals, local costumes and customs, different ways of living and getting around. It's up to you to match the words to the pictures! Don't worry if you can't find everything, because Gigi and Zachary have put the answers in the back of the book.

From north to south, east to west, it's all part of a grand adventure with Gigi and Zachary! Find out where their journey takes them.

Our going-away party on the African savanna

aardvark
antelope
cormorant
fire

fishing net
flamingo
gnu
hippopotamus

hut
hyena
jembe drum
kora harp

leopard
lion
lion cub
mandrill

mortar
obokano lyre
ostrich
pangolin

pestle
rhinoceros
river
spoonbill

talking drum
termite mound
warthog

Picking dates in an oasis in the Sahara

bedouin
binoculars
bundle
calabash
camel

cauldron
date palm
desert
desert fox
djellaba (garment)

donkey
dune
flask
garden
glass

goat
minaret
necklace
olive tree
rifle

ruins
salt block
scimitar
scorpion
teapot

tent pole
tent stake
tower
well

An opera singer in Venice

balcony	canal	cell phone	dome	guitar	mask	parasol	singer
boom operator	candelabra	chandelier	drum	gutter	microphone	prosciutto	straw boater
bouquet	carousel	clarinet	fountain	headphones	mouse	roof terrace	tourist
bridge	cask	clothesline	gargoyle	ice-cream cone	movie camera	salami	
camera	cat	conductor	gondola	lightbulb			

The port of Istanbul on the Bosphorus

bollard
cargo ship
container
crane

ferryboat
flag
forklift
gangway

jetty
landing stage
lighthouse
macaw

mosque
ocean liner
platform
seagull

quay
river
rolling door
sailboat

sailor
submarine
suspension bridge
tractor trailer

tugboat
warehouse

Trekking in the mountains of Tibet

backpack	glacier	monastery	sheep	sword	Tibetan trumpet	walking stick
cooking pot	kiang (wild donkey)	monk	Sherpa	tent	trunk	yak
drum	lynx	prayer wheel	Sherpa pack	Tibetan antelope	turban	
footbridge	masked dancer	rug	shrine	Tibetan oboe		

Riding an elephant in India

banana tree
banyan tree
boat
cobra

elephant
gavial (crocodile)
incense
ornamental pond

palace
plow
rice paddy
sari

sitar
snake charmer
tabla drums
tiger

train
tunnel
turban
water buffalo

water-drawer
yogi
zebu (ox)

A pedicab in Southeast Asia

ball	cart	gas pump	palm tree	satellite dish	street	utility pole
bicycle	coconut	goat	pedicab	scooter	streetcar	watermelon
billboard	cup	mason	pickup truck	service station	teapot	winch
brick oven	dominoes	mechanic	police officer	sidewalk	temple	
bus	donkey	motorcycle sidecar	refrigerator	sign	transistor radio	

Fishing in Indonesia

awning	coconut palm	fishing rod	jetty	pineapple	straw hat
canopy	crab	fishing trap	knife	sarong	volcano
cast net	dolphin	hornbill	mango	shrimp	
cockatoo	dugout canoe	house on pilings	mangrove		

A boxing match in Australia

Scuba diving in the South Pacific

anchor	diver propulsion	flying fish	lobster	propeller	sea star	spiny lobster
cannon	vehicle	gull	mast	ray	seaweed	sponge
coral	eel	hammerhead shark	mermaid	scallop	ship's wheel	sunfish
cuttlefish	figurehead	hermit crab	octopus	sea anemone	shipwreck	swordfish
	flippers	jellyfish	oxygen tank	sea horse	sperm whale	treasure

Carnival in Brazil

armadillo	cactus	cowbell	horse	mask	pennant	sugarcane
banner	cassava	earthworm	kite	oxcart	pig	television
bass drum	cattle	hoop	lasso	palm tree	rooster	top
birdcage	church	horn	maracas	parrot	sickle	

In the Amazon rain forest

anteater
arrow
boa constrictor
body painting

bow
butterfly
coati
feather headdress

hammock
heron
ibis
jaguar

loincloth
manatee
marmoset
orchid

parakeet
quiver
red ant
sloth

spear
tapir
toucan

vine
wild boar

In the marketplace in Guatemala

arum lily	basket weaver	candle	cloth bag	loom	stall
avocado	bell tower	church	coconut pieces	melon	stool
baby	bougainvillea	clay pot	ear of corn	panama hat seller	ziggurat
basket	broom	cloth	grinding wheel	potter	

Tightrope walking in Chicago

ambulance	elevated train	ice-cream	motor scooter	reporter	skateboard	stroller	traffic light
barrier	Ferris wheel	vendor	overpass	restaurant	skyscraper	supermarket	video camera
bus shelter	fire hydrant	ladder	parking garage	robot dog	storm drain	taxi	window washer
convertible	fire truck	manhole	pay phone	roller skates	street sweeper	tightrope	
crosswalk	helicopter	modern art	rat	roof terrace	streetlight	traffic cone	

white-water rafting in the Rocky Mountains

bear	coyote	hare	marmot	pine tree	rock climber
beaver	dam	honeybee	mountain lion	raccoon	salmon
bighorn sheep	doe	life jacket	opossum	raft	squirrel
canyon	elk	life ring	paddle	river	waterfall

Sledding in Alaska

auk

fishing trawler

harness

harpoon

husky

ice floe

iceberg

igloo

kayak

paddle

polar bear

puffin

scarf

seal

sled

snowmobile

snowshoes

walrus

whale

whip

Eating rice with chopsticks in China

bamboo	Chinese violin	dragon	ginkgo tree	pagoda	pelican	suitcase	track loader
bulldozer	concrete mixer	dump truck	grandfather	pail	rice bowl	tai chi	tricycle
cattail	crane	fishnet	Great Wall	panda	rug	teddy bear	wisteria
chef	dam	frog	lily pad	paper lantern	steam shovel	terraced hill	wok

A traveling caravan in Romania

accordion
awning
building
castanets

cell phone
clock
crystal ball
dancer

fortune-teller
grandmother
horse rider
jack

juggler
juggling balls
lace
mirror

playing cards
shutters
soccer ball
television

tent
toolbox
trailer
trumpet

TV antenna
violin
washtub
wrecked car

A farm in Poland

bale of hay	duck	goose	hose	mattock	owl	stork	turkey
calf	eggplant	greenhouse	ladder	melon	pitchfork	sunflower	water wheel
carrot	fence	harvester	lawnmower	milk jug	pruning shears	swallow	weather vane
chicken	field	hayloft	lettuce	mushroom	rabbit	tomato	wheelbarrow
church	footbridge	hoe	manger	orchard	shovel	tractor	windmill

our dream island

bench, grill, seaplane, treehouse…
and all the souvenirs that we brought back from our world tour!

Gigi and Zachary's tour of the world in 500 words

Our going-away party on the African savanna

1 aardvark
2 antelope
3 cormorant
4 fire
5 fishing net
6 flamingo
7 gnu
8 hippopotamus

9 hut
10 hyena
11 jembe drum
12 kora harp
13 leopard
14 lion
15 lion cub
16 mandrill
17 mortar
18 obokano lyre

19 ostrich
20 pangolin
21 pestle
22 rhinoceros
23 river
24 spoonbill
25 talking drum
26 termite mound
27 warthog

Picking dates in an oasis in the Sahara

1 bedouin
2 binoculars
3 bundle
4 calabash
5 camel
6 cauldron
7 date palm
8 desert
9 desert fox

10 djellaba
11 donkey
12 dune
13 flask
14 garden
15 glass

16 goat
17 minaret
18 necklace
19 olive tree
20 rifle
21 ruins
22 salt block
23 scimitar

24 scorpion
25 teapot
26 tent pole
27 tent stake
28 tower
29 well

An opera singer in Venice

1 balcony
2 boom operator
3 bouquet
4 bridge
5 camera
6 canal
7 candelabra
8 carousel
9 cask

10 cat
11 cell phone
12 chandelier
13 clarinet
14 clothesline
15 conductor
16 dome
17 drum
18 fountain
19 gargoyle
20 gondola
21 guitar
22 gutter
23 headphones

24 ice-cream cone
25 lightbulb
26 mask
27 microphone
28 mouse
29 movie camera
30 parasol
31 prosciutto
32 roof terrace
33 salami
34 singer
35 straw boater
36 tourist

The port of Istanbul on the Bosphorus

1. bollard
2. cargo ship
3. container
4. crane
5. ferryboat
6. flag
7. forklift
8. gangway
9. jetty
10. landing stage
11. lighthouse
12. macaw
13. mosque
14. ocean liner
15. platform
16. quay
17. river
18. rolling door
19. sailboat
20. sailor
21. seagull
22. submarine
23. suspension bridge
24. tractor trailer
25. tugboat
26. warehouse

Trekking in the mountains of Tibet

1. backpack
2. cooking pot
3. drum
4. footbridge
5. glacier
6. kiang (wild donkey)
7. lynx
8. masked dancer
9. monastery
10. monk
11. prayer wheel
12. rug
13. sheep
14. Sherpa
15. Sherpa pack
16. shrine
17. sword
18. tent
19. Tibetan antelope
20. Tibetan oboe
21. Tibetan trumpet
22. trunk
23. turban
24. walking stick
25. yak

Riding an elephant in India

1. banana tree
2. banyan tree
3. boat
4. cobra
5. elephant
6. gavial (crocodile)
7. incense
8. ornamental pond
9. palace
10. plow
11. rice paddy
12. sari
13. sitar
14. snake charmer
15. tabla drums
16. tiger
17. train
18. tunnel
19. turban
20. water buffalo
21. water-drawer
22. yogi
23. zebu (ox)

A pedicab in Southeast Asia

1. ball
2. bicycle
3. billboard
4. brick oven
5. bus
6. cart
7. coconut
8. cup
9. dominoes
10. donkey
11. gas pump
12. goat
13. mason
14. mechanic
15. motorcycle sidecar
16. palm tree
17. pedicab
18. pickup truck
19. police officer
20. refrigerator
21. satellite dish
22. scooter
23. service station
24. sidewalk
25. sign
26. street
27. streetcar
28. teapot
29. temple
30. transistor radio
31. utility pole
32. watermelon
33. winch

Fishing in Indonesia

1 awning
2 canopy
3 cast net
4 cockatoo
5 coconut palm
6 crab
7 dolphin
8 dugout canoe
9 fishing rod
10 fishing trap
11 hornbill
12 house on pilings
13 jetty
14 knife
15 mango
16 mangrove
17 pineapple
18 sarong
19 shrimp
20 straw hat
21 volcano

A boxing match in Australia

1 ant
2 boxer
3 boxing glove
4 boxing ring
5 cassowary
6 crocodile
7 dingo
8 dragonfly
9 echidna
10 emu
11 eucalyptus
12 gong
13 jeep
14 kangaroo
15 koala
16 monitor
17 phalanger
18 platypus
19 referee
20 rock painting
21 tree lizard
22 wallaby
23 whistle
24 wombat

Scuba diving in the South Pacific

1 anchor
2 cannon
3 coral
4 cuttlefish
5 diver propulsion vehicle
6 eel
7 figurehead
8 flippers
9 flying fish
10 gull
11 hammerhead shark
12 hermit crab
13 jellyfish
14 lobster
15 mast
16 mermaid
17 octopus
18 oxygen tank
19 propeller
20 ray
21 scallop
22 sea anemone
23 sea horse
24 sea star
25 seaweed
26 ship's wheel
27 shipwreck
28 sperm whale
29 spiny lobster
30 sponge
31 sunfish
32 swordfish
33 treasure

Carnival in Brazil

1 armadillo
2 banner
3 bass drum
4 birdcage
5 cactus
6 cassava
7 cattle
8 church
9 cowbell
10 earthworm

11 hoop
12 horn
13 horse
14 kite
15 lasso
16 maracas
17 mask
18 oxcart
19 palm tree

20 parrot
21 pennant
22 pig
23 rooster
24 sickle
25 sugarcane
26 television
27 top

In the Amazon rain forest

1 anteater
2 arrow
3 boa constrictor
4 body painting
5 bow
6 butterfly
7 coati
8 feather headdress
9 hammock
10 heron

11 ibis
12 jaguar
13 loincloth
14 manatee
15 marmoset
16 orchid
17 parakeet

18 quiver
19 red ant
20 sloth
21 spear
22 tapir
23 toucan
24 vine
25 wild boar

In the marketplace in Guatemala

1 arum lily
2 avocado
3 baby
4 basket
5 basket weaver
6 bell tower
7 bougainvillea
8 broom
9 candle
10 church

11 clay pot
12 cloth
13 cloth bag
14 coconut pieces
15 ear of corn
16 grinding wheel
17 loom

18 melon
19 panama hat seller
20 potter
21 stall
22 stool
23 ziggurat

Tightrope walking in Chicago

1 ambulance
2 barrier
3 bus shelter
4 convertible
5 crosswalk
6 elevated train
7 Ferris wheel
8 fire hydrant
9 fire truck
10 helicopter
11 ice-cream vendor
12 ladder
13 manhole

14 modern art
15 motor scooter
16 overpass
17 parking garage
18 pay phone
19 rat
20 reporter
21 restaurant
22 robot dog
23 roller skates
24 roof terrace

25 skateboard
26 skyscraper
27 storm drain
28 street sweeper
29 streetlight
30 stroller
31 supermarket
32 taxi
33 tightrope
34 traffic cone
35 traffic light
36 video camera
37 window washer

White-water rafting in the Rocky Mountains

1 bear
2 beaver
3 bighorn sheep
4 canyon
5 coyote
6 dam
7 doe
8 elk
9 hare
10 honeybee

11 life jacket
12 life ring
13 marmot
14 mountain lion
15 opossum
16 paddle
17 pine tree
18 raccoon

19 raft
20 river
21 rock climber
22 salmon
23 squirrel
24 waterfall

Sledding in Alaska

1 auk
2 fishing trawler
3 harness
4 harpoon
5 husky
6 ice floe
7 iceberg
8 igloo
9 kayak
10 paddle

11 polar bear
12 puffin
13 scarf
14 seal
15 sled
16 snowmobile
17 snowshoes
18 walrus
19 whale
20 whip

Eating rice with chopsticks in China

1 bamboo
2 bulldozer
3 cattail
4 chef
5 Chinese violin
6 concrete mixer

7 crane
8 dam
9 dragon
10 dump truck
11 fishnet
12 frog
13 ginkgo tree
14 grandfather
15 Great Wall
16 lily pad
17 pagoda
18 pail
19 panda
20 paper lantern

21 pelican
22 rice bowl
23 rug
24 steam shovel
25 suitcase
26 tai chi
27 teddy bear
28 terraced hill
29 track loader
30 tricycle
31 wisteria
32 wok

A traveling caravan in Romania

1. accordion
2. awning
3. building
4. castanets
5. cell phone
6. clock
7. crystal ball
8. dancer
9. fortune-teller

10. grandmother
11. horse rider
12. jack
13. juggler
14. juggling balls
15. lace
16. mirror
17. playing cards
18. shutters
19. soccer ball
20. television
21. tent

22. toolbox
23. trailer
24. trumpet
25. TV antenna
26. violin
27. washtub
28. wrecked car

A farm in Poland

1. bale of hay
2. calf
3. carrot
4. chicken
5. church
6. duck
7. eggplant
8. fence
9. field
10. footbridge

11. goose
12. greenhouse
13. harvester
14. hayloft
15. hoe
16. hose
17. ladder
18. lawnmower
19. lettuce
20. manger

21. mattock
22. melon
23. milk jug
24. mushroom
25. orchard
26. owl
27. pitchfork
28. pruning shears
29. rabbit
30. shovel

31. stork
32. sunflower
33. swallow
34. tomato
35. tractor
36. turkey
37. water wheel
38. weather vane
39. wheelbarrow
40. windmill

Our dream island

1. bench
2. boxing glove
3. Carnival mask
4. cast net
5. clay pot
6. cloth
7. diving mask
8. dominoes
9. feather headdress
10. grill

11. lace
12. ladder
13. life ring
14. macaw
15. oxygen tank
16. paper lantern
17. parasol
18. puffin
19. rice bowl
20. seaplane

21. shovel
22. straw boater
23. tabla drums
24. teapot
25. traffic cone
26. treasure chest
27. treehouse